Dear Mr. President ™

Winslow Press wishes to acknowledge the following sources for the photographs and illustrations in this book:

Library, American Museum of Natural History, p. 23 (negative #2A6155)

Library of Congress, Prints and Photographs Division, cover photo, pp. 4, 6, 7, 8, 9, 10, 11, 12, 14, 15, 17, 19, 21, 25, 26, 27, 28, 30, 31, 32–33, 35, 39, 42–43, 45, 47, 48, 50–51, 54, 55, 56–57, 62, 65, 66, 67 (cartoon detail), 70, 72, 75, 79, 82, 85, 88, 91, 93, 95, 96, 98

Sagamore Hill National Historic Site, pp. 41, 46

Schuylkill County Historical Society, Pottsville, PA, pp. 53, 61, 81

Line drawings on pages 18 and 68-69, were drawn by Theodore Roosevelt in letters to his children, and are taken from the book *Theodore Roosevelt's Letters to His Children* (New York: Scribner's, 1919). The illustrated letter on pg. 111 is also taken from that book.

Cover illustration © 2000 by Mark Summers

DEAR MR. PRESIDENT and the DEAR MR. PRESIDENT logo are registered trademarks of Winslow Press.

Thanks to R. Sean Wilentz, Dayton-Stockton Professor of History and Director, Program in American Studies, Princeton University, for evaluating the manuscript.

Armstrong, Jennifer, 1961–
Theodore Roosevelt: letters from a young coal miner / written by Jennifer Armstrong.—1st ed.
p. cm.—(Dear Mr. President)
Includes biographical references and index.
Summary: Thirteen-year-old Frank Kovacs, a Polish immigrant working in the coal mines of eastern Pennsylvania, begins a correspondence with Theodore Roosevelt after he assumes the presidency on September 14, 1901.

ISBN: 1-890817-27-9
1. Roosevelt, Theodore, 1858-1919—Juvenile fiction. [1. Roosevelt, Theodore, 1858-1919—Fiction. 2. Coal mines and mining—Fiction. 3. Immigrants—Fiction. 4. Polish Americans—Fiction. 5. Letters—Fiction.] I. Title.
PZ7.A73367 Tj 2000
[Fic]-dc21

Creative Director: Bretton Clark
Designer: David Pelletier
Editor: Margery Cuyler

Printed in Belgium
First Edition
10 9 8 7 6 5 4 3 2 1

Dear Mr. President

Theodore Roosevelt
Letters from a Young Coal Miner

by Jennifer Armstrong

WINSLOW PRESS

Florida • New York

A Note From the Publisher

With this book, we are introducing our *Dear Mr. President* series. The text is in the form of letters passed back and forth between President Theodore Roosevelt and a coal mining boy. Although the letters are fictional, the information in them is based on meticulous research. In an effort to capture President Roosevelt's personality, as well as the history of the coal strike of 1902, the author relied on *A Bully Father: Theodore Roosevelt's Letters to His Children*, *The Kingdom of Coal: Work, Enterprise, and Ethnic Communities in the Mine Fields*, and other reputable books. The character of Frank Kovacs evolved from reading Susan Campbell Bartoletti's invaluable work, *Growing Up In Coal Country*, as well as primary source material such as that provided by "Coal Mining in the Gilded Age and Progressive Era," an on-line project of The Ohio State University Department of History. A list of recommended reading can be found on pages 108-109. Watch for prompts at the bottom of the pages.

We hope that readers will gain valuable insights into important moments of American history from reading our *Dear Mr. President* books. Written by a skilled author, each title is further enhanced by interactive games, activities, links, and detailed historical information found in our virtual library, winslowpress.com.

By offering you a rich reading experience coupled with our interactive Web site, we encourage you to embrace the future with what is best from the past.

Diane F. Kessenich, Publisher and CEO, Winslow Press

Young workers around the ages 9 to 15, from the Pennsylvania coal mines at the beginning of the 20th century. The men shown in the background probably worked with the boys because they had been injured.

Dear Mr.President,

Sincerely,

Frank Kovacs

Dear Mr. Kovacs,

Sincerely,

Theodore Roosevelt

Introduction

At the turn of the twentieth century, the industrial cities of the eastern United States ran on anthracite coal. From Bangor, Maine to Norfolk, Virginia, factories and homes burned this soft, black fuel dug from underground mines.

America was entering the century with glowing enthusiasm. The only thing that darkened this brave new horizon was thick clouds of coal smoke and a fine rain of soot. Sweeping twice a day was a necessity in some cities. People had to change their clothes if they strayed too close to belching smokestacks and chimneys.

The industrial states were driving America into the forefront of world commerce and power. The fuel that kept the fires hot was coal: black gold. But who brought that black gold up from underground? Who dug the coal that fueled America? This was hard, brutal work at low pay, in parts of Pennsylvania where the living conditions were poor and difficult. By and large, the only people who would take these toilsome jobs and live in these impoverished towns were the new Americans, the immigrants pouring through Ellis Island day after day. Poles, Lithuanians, Germans,

This building, called a breaker, was where coal was sorted by boys. The chute in the foreground carried processed coal down to the smaller buildings on the left.

To learn more about immigration, visit winslowpress.com.

Hungarians, Slovakians, Silesians and Czechs made their way to the coal patch of Pennsylvania. They came in search of new lives in a new land, and they burrowed right into its very heart.

Imagine a boy named Frank Kovacs who lives in the coal patch with his family. Imagine him having to quit school to go to work in the mines. His life would have been difficult. He would have had a hard time keeping up with his reading and writing practice. But he would know that in America, everyone has the right to send a letter to the president. Imagine that Frank Kovacs wrote to Theodore Roosevelt, who became the 26th president of the United States of America in September, 1901.

These young miners, called spraggers, are holding onto the stick or sprag that they used for slowing the coal cars. They would jam the stick between the spokes of the wheels.

Immigrants looking across New York harbor at the New World after landing at Ellis Island.

September 20, 1901

Oneida, Pennsylvania
Dear Mr. Roosevelt,

I heard at work about that President McKinley got gunned down by a crazy fellow and now you are president instead of vice president. It is an important job.

But I have advice for you and that is don't let no crazy men near you. They is almost always trouble.

Wishing you health and good luck,

Frank Kovacs

Frank Kovacs

For more information on the
assassination of McKinley,
visit winslowpress.com

September 27, 1901

The White House

Dear Mr. Kovacs,

Thank you very much for your congratulatory letter and your wishes for good luck, and for your very sound advice. I promise to do my level best at this job. It is a great honor for me to be leading this great country into the twentieth century. The future is limitless.

I'm always glad to hear from the working men of this great country of ours. Men like you have the common sense that many over-educated folks never learn. I shall indeed strive to keep clear of lunatics and assassins.

Sincerely yours,

Theodore Roosevelt

Theodore Roosevelt

Oneida, Pennsylvania

Dear Mr. President

   I don't wish to let you continue in a mistaken thought. I ain't a working-man. Leastways, I work but I am not full growed yet. But I do work at the colliery. I heard the miners talking about how President McKinley got killed and that made you the president, but I wanted to tell you I ain't exactly a man yet.

Sincerely,

Frank Kovacs

Frank Kovacs

Young miners left school around fifth grade to work in the mines.

October 14, 1901

The White House

Dear Master Kovacs,

Thank you very much for clearing up my misperception. I found your first letter, and I must admit that I leapt to conclusions because you said you heard "at work." We're very busy learning the ropes here in the White House, and things are a bit confusing, as you might well imagine, and I have a habit of working very fast. So I am grateful that someone like you is willing to speak up when I'm getting ahead of myself and making a mistake. You would be surprised how many people let the title "president" dazzle them into silence, no matter how much of a confounded fool I'm being. Much like the Emperor's new clothes, if you see what I mean.

So you're not fully grown up yet, in spite of working at the colliery. How old are you? And what work do you do in the mine? I would very much like to know.

Sincerely,

Theodore Roosevelt

Theodore Roosevelt

To learn more about collieries, visit winslowpress.com.

October 22, 1901

Oneida, Pennsylvania

Dear Mr. President,

I don't know who that Emperor is you mentioned or what his clothes is like but you asked me how old I am and so I'll tell you I am 15 years old and I work in Coxe Brothers Number 2 mine at Oneida tending the mules. They is important to the mine seeing as to how they pull the cars full of coal. Caring for these mules, this is an important job. They eat alfalfa corn oats, also carrots and apples. Also they will eat anything else they can get a hold on, for instance your own lunch if you are careless with it. We brush them and we make repairs to the harnesses.

A fellow I know read out of the newspaper the other day saying you love horses. I love horses too but all we got here is mules. They are good workers but stubborn. And they is smart too, did you know that? Even when they can't hear the whistle at quitting time they know when the day is done, and they just stop wherever they are. The driver has

got to
unhitch the cars,
'cause that mule won't
pull no more that day, not for
twenty apples. A man I know once
had to singe his mule's belly with
a carbide lamp to get him up and
moving again.

I expect you are a very educated
man to be chosen president and
it may be you can solve a riddle
for me. Why do they call this the
twentieth century when it starts
with 19? I did not get to finish
my schooling and it may be that
they explained this part of
arithmetic after I left.

Sincerely,

Frank Kovacs

Frank Kovacs

To learn more about mules in the mines, visit winslowpress.com.

The mules shown above were fortunate enough to get some fresh air. Most mules spent their lives underground.

The White House

Dear Master Kovacs,

Yes, indeed, I do love horses. Right now I like to ride a big fellow named Bleistein. We go for many a ramble around Washington, especially at night when the moon is shining. That's a fine spectacle.

Mrs. Roosevelt is also a superb horsewoman, and I've taught all my children to ride. My son Archie is very good now at riding our calico pony, Algonquin, who is a sweet-tempered animal, but has been known to play tricks. He often wanders loose on the lawn, and is very good at sneaking up behind any child who happens to be there: then he'll nudge and nudge and nudge with his nose until the poor small person is in a hedge. He's also fond of stopping short and letting his rider fly off over his head. Archie takes his knocks like a brave fellow, I'm glad to say. He says it doesn't hurt much more than being in a pillow fight—which is a common sort of war in this house.

Watch those mules: they've got more tricks in them than ten Algonquins.

As for the riddle of the century, well, there was a whole century's worth of years before we got to year 100, which is considered the first century. So the one hundred years that came after 100 are called the second century. I was born in 1858, that is, in the 19th century. I hope that clears up the confusion.

Sincere regards,

Theodore Roosevelt

To learn more about "child's play" in the White House, visit winslowpress.com.

Archie, President Roosevelt's third son, on his pony, Algonquin.

19

Oneida, Pennsylvania

Dear Mr. President,

I do thank you for explaining that business about the centuries. If I hadn't a left school so young maybe I'd a known that myself. But now I do understand it. I guess I was born in the 19th century as well.

Yes, you are right, them mules have their tricks. One thing they like to do is squeeze you. If you're in a tight tunnel and you have to come up past them, they will try to press you against the wall. An elbow in the ribs usually does the job, though, or like I say, a bit of a singe with a lamp. Also we got these sticks, we call them sprags, that are for sticking into the wheelspokes for slowing the cars down. You can jab a mule with a sprag and it moves on real smart after that. Also you can sometime pore a little water into there ears and their do not like that at all so they will get going.

I do sometimes feel sorry for them. The mine mules live down in the mine. We've got stables cut right into the rock, and the mules just live down underground. We send their feed, also water, down on the coal cars, and take the manure out the same way. Once a mine mule gets let out into the outside, there ain't no power on earth that'll get it down underground

again. I don't say I blame 'em. Sometimes
I think there ain't no power that'll get
me down underground again myself. But I
have to do it, every day. Have been for
three years now. I get up at five-thirty
in the dark and go to work where it's dark
and come home when it's dark except in the
summer when it stays light late. I guess I
know how them mules feel once they get to
see the sunshine again. You hate to go
back where it's dark.

Sincerely,

Frank Kovacs

Frank Kovacs

*The mules were called "The Sweethearts of the Mine" and were
treated well by the boys.*

November 12, 1901

The White House

Dear Master Kovacs,

I recall you said you're fifteen. And you've been in the mines three years already? I'm sure you're doing right by your family, but I feel a great sympathy for you. You're the same age as my Ted, Jr., who is away at boarding school in Massachusetts. I wouldn't like to think about him being down in a coal mine day after day. A boy must have fresh air and sunshine. I hope you have your time to be a boy. My advice to you is stick to your school books and then go to work when you're a bit older.

Also, I don't think the air underground can be very healthful. You must be sure to take exercise regularly. Boxing matches, running, hiking, football: these are all good wholesome ways for a boy to spend his time.

Sincerely,

Theodore Roosevelt

Theodore Roosevelt

To learn more about Sagamore Hill, visit winslowpress.com.

Theodore Roosevelt playing ball with his children on the lawn at Sagamore Hill, his home in Oyster Bay, New York.

November 20, 1901

Oneida, Pennsylvania
Dear Mr. President,

I did say I am fifteen but that was a lie, I am thirteen. I started working in the Oneida coal breaker when I was eight, and then I got this better job. But I had to lie about my age. My family needed the money.

Working in the breaker ain't such a good job anyway. Breaker boys has to sit over the coal shoots and pick out pieces of slate and rock from the coal as it goes by, and the bosses don't let the boys wear gloves even when it's real cold and even though the sulfur on the coal makes your fingers bleed. Goose grease helps but that still don't make the job a better job. And also that breaker is loud as thunder, and a boy can't hear himself thinking his own thoughts. Your boy that is at boarding school is a lucky boy, and I hope he knows it. I guess a boarding school is real quiet. On account I had to leave off my schooling, I been trying to keep up as good as I can and I do read the Bible and the newspapers and I can sound them out pretty good. I also do any writing what my mama or papa needs and I take a look at my sisters school books from time to time if I ain't too tired at night. I wish I could have more schooling but that ain't going to happen.

We do have games on Sundays. After mass we have baseball, also wrestling and also running races. On the other days from the week, we are working from early morning until night.

Sincerely,

Frank Kovacs

Frank Kovacs

To learn more about school life in a mining town **and also the role of** breaker boys **in the** colliery, visit winslowpress.com.

The boys shown above are working in a coal breaker.

25

November 28, 1901

The White House

Dear Master Frank Kovacs,

Now I am very sorry. I look at my son Kermit, who right now is teaching his dog Skip how to bark when Kermit says "Speech, speech!" (A joke aimed at his father.) Kermit is thirteen.

Why is it that such a young fellow as you must be working in the mines? And why do you say that you can't have any more schooling? Education is a right granted to every child in this land. I don't understand.

Sincerely,

Theodore Roosevelt

A real-life adolescent coal miner, after whom the character Frank Kovacs is modeled.

Kermit Roosevelt at about age 15.

December 6, 1901

Oneida, Pennsylvania

Dear Mr. President

You asked why I had to be working and so I'll tell you. My mother and father came here from the old  country before I was born. They're Poles from Silesia, but since I was born in Pennsylvania, that makes me a true and true American, like you although I also call myself a Pole because I am proud of that. Father got good work in the mines and took care of all us kids the best he could, but he was hurt pretty bad last summer in a rockfall. His leg got broke and it never did heal right. The company don't give a man anything if he can't work, even when he got hurt working for the company. It don't seem right to me, but that's how it is. Seeing as I'm the oldest which I got two sisters and two brothers all younger than me I got to help out.

Mama and Mila and Janka who is my sisters pick coal out of the culm heaps and sell it in town, which is a help. Them culm heaps is where the leftover bits of rock and such get throwed out from the breaker. There is always some coal bits what get mixed in. But most everything we buy we got to buy at the company store. They take it right out of my wages, and sometimes when I get my pay, there ain't more than a few cents left over to give to Mama.

Also, the company is taking out of my wages to pay for some equipment that got broke when my Papa had his accident. And Mama says there will be a new baby soon.

That is why I work in the mine.

Sincerely,

Frank Kovacs

Frank Kovacs

Between 1880 and 1920, more than 20 million immigrants came to the United States.

To learn more about mining accidents visit winslowpress.com.

29

The White House

Dear Frank,

When you say "the company" I guess you mean the coal company. I've heard of this practice. They run the company store, and no doubt they also own the house you live in, and they can charge whatever prices and rents they want because they've got the only game in town. I think it is an outrage.

The coal miners of Pennsylvania are the engine that runs America. Without your sweat and toil, our factories would close, the trains would cease to run, the lights would go out and we'd all be frozen come winter. Why, in Washington it is so cold out right now you can see your breath, but here in the White House it is snug and warm, thanks to coal that might very well have come from your mine. It's a considerable sorrow to me to know how poorly you are treated.

I have read your letters to Mrs. Roosevelt, and she shares my sentiments. She thinks something should be done on behalf of the miners, and so do I. By the way you write I can tell you are an intelligent and enterprising young man. Do keep up your reading and writing: it will always be useful to you and can help you improve your circumstances in the future.

In this season of joy and cheer, I wish you and your family all the very best. Our thoughts are with you.

Your friend,

Theodore Roosevelt

Theodore Roosevelt

To learn more about the coal companies, visit winslowpress.com.

Miners with their lunch pails exiting from a shaft elevator. The carbide lamps on their hats lit the way.

Oneida Pennsylvania

Dear Mr. Roosevelt,

Thank you. Happy Christmas greetings to you and your family. And while I'm at it, Happy New Year, too. I did not wish to upset you by my last letter. I won't mention the hardsomeness any more, nor I won't write no more either if you don't like it. I didn't intend to be a bother.

Happy Christmas,

Frank Kovacs

Frank Kovacs

To see more photos and learn about President Roosevelt's family, visit winslowpress.com.

33

Theodore and Edith (seated) with their children. From left to right: Quentin, Theodore Jr., Archie, Alice, Kermit, and Ethel

January 2, 1902

Sagamore Hill
Oyster Bay, Long Island
Dear Frank,

You put me to shame. I enjoy your letters very much, and I would be very glad to hear all about your work and your family and what happens in the mine.

We are all here at our own home in New York, and it is always a great joy to be surrounded by family. My children are all with me: Alice, who is 18, Ted, 14, Kermit, 12, Ethel—our little mother—is 10, Archie is 8 and Quentin is 4. The last two young people are underfoot even as I write this, using my feet as some sort of landmark in a game they've devised. We had a splendid holiday, and are steeling ourselves to return to Washington. It is hard to leave the pleasantness of our home here; our house is very warm with family and with great fires of logs in the fireplaces. But we also have a coal furnace and for that I thank you and your fellow miners in Pennsylvania. When I was a lad we made a great game of sliding down the coal chute into the cellar, and, of course, our clothes and our faces and hands got thoroughly blackened. It was a devil of a job to get clean: I know you face this every day when you go underground. I know it is perhaps the least of the hardships you have to bear, but when I think how completely you must entomb yourself in the earth so that I can stay warm, it humbles me and makes me wish to return to my work and always strive to do a better job.

Sincerely,

Theodore Roosevelt

Theodore Roosevelt

Quentin and Archie blowing bubbles at Sagamore Hill.

The mines were damp and poorly lit.

January 11, 1902

Oneida, Pennsylvania

Dear Mr. Roosevelt,

You ain't far wrong about coal dirt. My mama makes me take my clothes off outside the house even when it's real cold. Even though I do that we still get the coal dirt into the house. I guess its just everywhere in the air around these parts. And it ain't easy to clean up at all. I don't guess my hands is ever clean no matter what I do. I did once see a picture of heaven, and all the angels was wearing white clothes and standing around on clean white clouds and such. I suppose they don't let no miners into heaven on account of we would dirty up the place right fast. I hope that don't mean miners got to go to the other place. We spend plenty of time below in this life already. This is a joke I am making and I hope it ain't a rude one or that it gets your back hairs up.

We had a bang-up Christmas, too. The mine let out early on Christmas eve, and some of us boys had a snowball fight on the way home that was mighty like a war. One of the breaker boys threw a snowball at the breaker boss and knocked his hat clean off, and the boss couldn't tell which boy did it so nobody got in trouble.

When I got home, my mama was cooking the goose that she'd been fattening up with potato peels and corn since summer. We had also pickled cabbage with that roasted goose. Also potatoes and some mushrooms Mila picked in the woods and made into pierogies. Not all mushrooms you can eat, but Mila is a smart girl she knows the good ones. Pierogies is a kind of dumpling, I don't know if you ever ate any.

We did put some hay on the table for the symbol of Jesus Christ's manger and we went to mass at midnight. The temperature was very bitter. My little brothers that I believe I mentioned to you fell asleep in the mass, and we had to carry them home. They are of the names Stepan and Tadek which is how in the Polish language we say the names Steven and Teddy. Mama says that we must be American now except she don't speak the American language too good. Sometimes she forgets to say Steven or Teddy and she says instead Stepan or Tadek. She said to me that if the new baby will be a boy, she will call his name Billy. She says that is the most American name she does know.

For a Christmas gift I got a pair of wool socks and an orange. That was the first orange I ever ate. It was sure good.

I did not know you had so many children. Like us it is a big family.

Your friend,

Frank Kovacs

Frank Kovacs

For more information on Polish Christmas customs, visit winslowpress.com.

37

January 20, 1902

The White House

Dear Frank,

I'm very glad to know you have a Ted in the family. We've got two, Ted Junior and myself. I think Teds are indispensable! I'm sorry that yours did not have the endurance for the midnight mass, but, as you say, he had to be carried home. He must be a very small Ted indeed. Much can be forgiven of very small Teds. And I'm glad as well to hear that your marksman friend who hit the target (I mean the breaker boss) went undetected. Boys must have their fun, and we big persons must be the butt of jokes from time to time and be good sports about it. My own sons are notorious with beanshooters here in the White House and take particular delight in hitting the shining bald head of one of our telegraph operators: I am afraid he doesn't have the sportsmanlike grace to laugh it off, which only makes my boys stalk him again. If he would only learn to joke with them and make friends they would like him too much and look for other prey.

How pleasant for you to have an orange as a Christmas treat. I'm very fond of oranges, myself. When I was in Cuba in '98 we ate them all the time. Cuba seems very far away and long ago now. At the moment, we're having a hard freeze in Washington, and it's hard to imagine the world

ever being green
and warm again.
I thoroughly
enjoyed your joke
about the miners
in heaven and
even shared it
with Mrs.
Roosevelt, and
you can be
sure I would
not have
done so if it
had been a rude one. I'd say that
considering all the time miners spend "down
below," that they certainly do deserve a home in heaven,
no matter how bad their sins!

I understand it never gets very cold underground.
Is that so?

Your friend,

Theodore Roosevelt

Theodore Roosevelt

P.S. In rereading your letter I see you ask if I ever ate pierogies. Yes
indeed, I have! I grew up in New York City where there are many
restaurants for people from all over Europe. Lüchows was always my
favorite, and they serve all sorts of hearty German and Polish fare. I
should say I have eaten pierogies, and enjoyed them very much!

For an anecdote about one Christmas at the White House,
visit winslowpress.com.

*Theodore Roosevelt with his
wife, Edith Carow Roosevelt.*

February 28, 1902

Oneida, Pennsylvania

Dear Mr. President,

   You asked if it gets cold underground and the answer is no, it don't. The temperature stays pretty even all year around. Not exactly warm, but not cold. Also it is damp in feeling. And seeing as how I work around the mules, I stay pretty snug. When I did work in the breaker it was raw and bitter work which is from the breaker being up overground and not heated at all hardly. Them breaker boys is cold all winter long.

   One of my mules, Button, stepped on a rat's leg yesterday when I was feeding him. The rat's leg got broke, and I felt bad for him on account of that's what happened to my Papa. So even though that rat was stealing Button's food, I'm trying to heal him up. I do always carry a lump of sugar or extra piece of bis-cuit for Button in my pocket but now I do give part of it to this rat to make him strong. Button I think will not like this very much. He did try to eat my hat.

   And please tell me what does that mean, P.S.?

From your friend,

Frank Kovacs

Frank (Kovacs)

The White House

Dear Frank,

Did you know we've got a rat here in the White House? It's my son Quentin's pet, by name of Jonathan, and he is a devil. He (the rat, not Quentin) bit the French ambassador one day, and if we don't go to war with France over it, I'll consider myself a lucky man. Quentin apologized, of course. The rat did not.

I think it's good and kind of you to look out for that creature. God made all of us, large and small, and your rat was only trying to eat like the rest of us.

How is your father? Is his leg getting any better? It must be a hard thing for him to see his children working when he cannot. As I think I mentioned in another letter, I've got six children myself, and I would hate to find myself unable to care for them.

Affectionately,

Theodore Roosevelt

P.S. P.S. means post script, which is a fancy way of saying "Oh, and one other thing I meant to tell you" after you've already signed your name.

While Quentin had a tame rat, Archie's favorite pet was a badger named Josiah. Roosevelt described him as "fundamentally friendly" even though his "temper was short."

41

Oneida, Pennsylvania

Dear Mr. Roosevelt,

My pa, his leg still ain't quite right but he can hobble around pretty good. He thinks he maybe could go back to the mine, but I doubt he'll ever be a miner again. That's a job it takes two good legs and two good arms. He could maybe work as a fire boss. That does mean he would be first man in the mine each day, checking for gas or for weak roofs and then tell the fellows when it was safe or not. If he can tolerate that much walking about on his gimpy leg, he might do that job.

Last week my mama had a fever cold and my papa said she spent too much time outside in the cold wind getting coal from the culm heaps. He said she didn't have any call to get sick and make things harder on him. She didn't talk back to him on account of her old country ways but I told Papa she worked hard as two miners. Maybe he could take a turn picking the culm heaps, seeing as how he only sits around inside during the day and says the cold makes his leg hurt. I know it is awful hard on a man not to be able to work, and I hope I wasn't too much disrespectful. But I was sore on account of my mama not having a fever to spite him and also the new baby inside her making her tired.

I hope it ain't a insult to you, but I call my rat Roosevelt. Seeing as how you like rats, I guess you won't take it wrong. His leg is healing up good. Plus he eats out of my hand like a pet puppy dog. I let him sleep inside my tin lunch pail after he finishes the crumbs of my lunch. One of the other boys that works here, his name is Joe. He saw Roosevelt in my pail and hollered so loud he spooked the mules. When I said to him, is he afraid of rats?, he said he ain't afraid of rats only he was surprised. I think he is afraid in truth.

Your friend,

Frank Kovacs

Frank (Kovacs)

March 23, 1902

The White House

Dear Frank,

I am heartily glad that your father may be able to return to work. Perhaps if he does, you will be able to return to school. I hope so. I'd like to see you out of the mine. I know it's a dangerous place—for man, boy and beast.

And I think you are right in thinking that it is being unable to support his family that makes your father cross. Be a good patient son, and remember to honor your father. It is better to shoulder the extra burden without complaint than to call attention to the weakness of another. This is a rule I have tried very hard to teach my sons, and I suggest it to you as a good line to follow.

Remember also to be kind and helpful to your mother while she is in her delicate condition. You want your little brother Billy to be healthy. Mrs. Roosevelt sends as a message to your mother the advice to rest as often as possible and drink milk. We Roosevelts have seen our share of babies. They are a joy and a blessing to all. My daughter Ethel is a regular "little mother" to her pets and her brothers and says that what babies like best is plenty of brothers and sisters about.

Your friend,

Theodore Roosevelt

Theodore Roosevelt

2.R. V.P

PLEASE
DON'TSCARE
BIRDS

SHUT
THIS DOOR
THAT MEANS YOU

*One of the most dangerous and lonely jobs was that of a nipper. He
had to open and close the door to the passageways deep inside the
coal mine. The doors acted as valves to route fresh air to different
parts of the mine. If the nipper's timing was off, he could be crushed
by an oncoming coal car.*

March 31, 1902

Oneida, Pennsylvania

Dear Mr. President,

I aim to keep working even if my pa goes back on the job. I was working before he ever got hurt anyway. Plus I got promoted to driver. Button is who I drive. He can pull four cars and he's so smart he knows if you try to hitch on five. Also he knows this mine good. I got lost yesterday, but Button he knew

just where to go so I let him have the reins and he just found his way back to the gangway. His ears is all blunted at the tips from rubbing along the roof of the shafts, but those ears tell him when he's got to duck his head. He's a real smart mule.

It ain't all bad here. The union is trying to get better conditions

Ethel and Kermit with their nanny, Mame, riding in a pony cart.

for us. They're aiming to get us better wages and a shorter work day. Plus, they want a change in the way the coal gets weighed — which is how a miner knows how much he's earned at the end of a week. The bosses usually say there is a ton or so of rock mixed in with the coal, so they don't even count that. Never mind if a miner is careful to make sure there ain't nothing but coal in the wagon.

There was a union meeting over at Shamokin just a week or so. That's what I heard, anyway. (Shamokins a town west of here.) And if the coal companies don't agree to the union demands, they say there may be a strike.

Greetings from Your friend Frank

Frank

P.S. My mama has too many work to do for resting. Also milk costs very much money for us. But Mila and Janka do help her. Monday it is the washing day, then Tuesday for the ironing, Wednesday they do baking, Thursday it is for sewing and mending, Friday it is for cleaning house, Saturday when is pay day is for shopping and having a bath and Sunday is for God. This is why you can see it is not too much time for resting.

Mules quickly learned their way through the mines.

To learn more about what life was like for girls in a mining town, visit winslowpress.com.

The White House

Dear Frank,

I would be very sorry if the miners decide to strike. I know that the big companies try to get away with treating their workers poorly. I have never been a booster for big business, but have always prided myself on looking out for the working man. But I'm sure there's a better way of resolving differences. I don't approve of work stoppages. And how would your mother fare if you have to stop work? If you are the only member of your family bringing in wages, it will be very difficult for her. Take my advice and stick at your work.

On Sunday I rounded up as many children as I could lay my hands on and led a long scramble through Rock Creek Park here in Washington. This is our habitual Sunday excursion, and sometimes we have as many as fifteen or sixteen small people along, be they schoolmates of my children or the children of friends and White House staff. This drives the Secret Service police who are assigned to protect me nearly to distraction, as trying to keep up with a mob of youngsters is akin to trying to push a wheelbarrow full of frogs. They never do know which direction we might be headed in.

Write to me again, and let me know how you're getting on.

Your friend,

Theodore Roosevelt

Theodore Roosevelt

This cartoon shows the coal companies, depicted by the men in top hats, denying that they are keeping the price of coal artificially high. Roosevelt is portrayed as a bear.

To learn more about the origins of the teddy bear, named for Theodore Roosevelt, visit winslowpress.com

49

Oneida, Pennsylvania

Dear Mr. President,

My sisters Mila and Janka did paint eggs for Easter, these eggs we call pisanky. These are traditional Polish design. Mila and Janka sold them at church for one penny each before Easter and did make enough money to buy five pounds sugar and flour and then made many cookies. We ate some but then they sold these cookies at church and did earn enough from that to buy a one dozen duck eggs to brood. When those ducks hatch we will for sure have a lot of noise.

The union people say there's going to be a strike for sure. Most of us families keep pigs and geese and also a garden, and my mama grew up on a farm in Silesia so she knows all there is to know about growing potatoes and cabbage and the like. I don't guess we'll starve if we have to go off work to get what's fair. Don't you think we ought to stand up for what we think is fair? I did say to Mama what you told me about her and she said to me that she wants the strike for fairness.

Frank Kovacs

Frank Kovacs

This cartoon shows President Roosevelt encouraging a miner to shake hands with a coal company operator.

To learn more about Polish Easter customs, visit winslowpress.com.

51

April 30, 1902

The White House

Dear Frank,

Your mother sounds as though she is a very brave and resourceful woman, and I'm happy to know that you won't starve if worse comes to worse. And if your sisters don't end up as wealthy capitalists, I shall be very surprised! They seem to have the hang of business, all right! The ducks will make plenty of noise, but when it comes time to eat them you'll forget how tiresome they were and enjoy every bite.

And yes, I do think a man should stand up and demand his fair due. That's one of the duties of manly dignity. But I repeat, I do not approve of work stoppages and strikes. The miners and the mine owners must learn to resolve their disagreements through discussion and negotiation. These extreme measures cannot be successful.

Your friend,

Theodore Roosevelt

Theodore Roosevelt

Woman and children in an old mining town.

May 11, 1902

Oneida, Pennsylvania

Dear Mr. President,

Roosevelt is getting along pretty good. He don't hardly limp at all now. Folks around here is pretty edgy. Even Button knows. Down in the mine, when the roof starts making noise we say it's working. You have to listen close in case it works too much and maybe will come down or come a cave in. That's what it feels like now: the whole mine is working, only it ain't the roof, it's the miners.

The strike is called for tomorrow. The union won't be calling out the maintenance people—the men that operates the pumps to keep the mines dry, and boys that has to look after the mules. But no miner will go to work tomorrow. The union president, that's Johnny Mitchell, he's been trying and trying to get the coal companies to move even the slightest inch on giving the coal workers a better deal. Only they won't.

To find out more about John Mitchell, visit winslowpress.com.

The coal companies is being stub-
borner than mules. But miners can be
stubbornest of all. I try to see what
you say about the duties of manly
dignity. I know you're the president
and a educated man, and I am nothing
but a kid that never went to school
more than a little bit. But ain't it
the duty of manly dignity to say he
won't be treated like dirt? Or like
he ain't got no more feelings than a
machine? Seems to me he wouldn't be
a man to have any dignity if he let
the rich company owners turn him
into a machine.

Your friend,

Frank Kovacs

Frank K.
p.s. Them ducks did hatch and they follow Mila everywhere she goes.

May 20, 1902

The White House

Dear Frank,

Well, I am sorry about the strike. I have expressed my opinion on that. But I'm curious to know how you and your family will get along with no wages coming in? You must get milk for your mother if you can.

I'm also very concerned at reports I've heard about violence against non-union workers. Have you seen anything of this nature? I trust you will keep yourself well out of it.

My son Archie declares that if there is trouble, he'll be glad to "lend a hand." He considers himself a member of the White House police squad, and answers roll call every morning with them. As he is only eight years old, however, I don't think I'll send him down.

With best wishes,

Theodore Roosevelt

Theodore Roosevelt

Archie and Quentin with White House policemen.

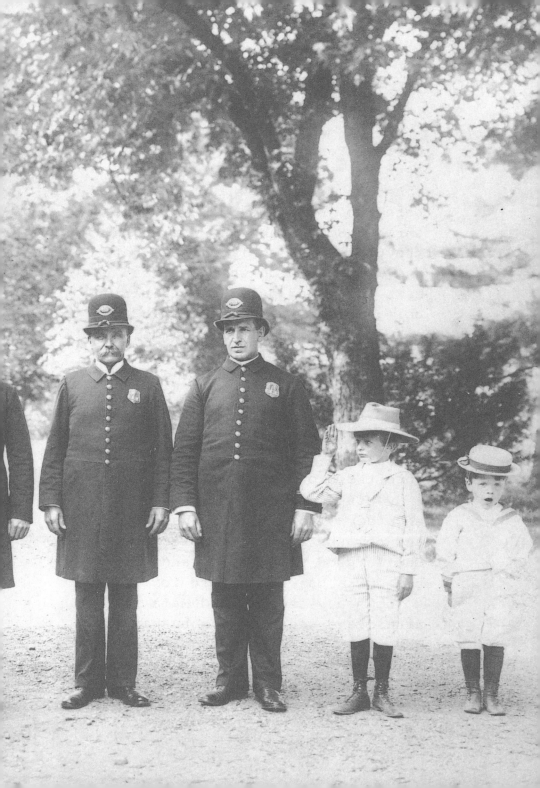

May 26, 1902

Oneida, Pennsylvania

Dear Mr. President,

Let me tell you what happened here two years ago during the last strike. Some scabs was working at the Oneida and strikers from here and from Sheppton which is just the next town, had a big demonstration going outside the mine and it was peaceful with families and old people and all. There was some yelling, but nobody getting beat up or throwing rocks. There was a whole bunch of company police guarding the breaker, and without no warning they started shooting into the crowd.

My sister Mila got hit in the shoulder with a bullet that day and now she's got a crooked arm. She is good with baking and with the ducks but it is hard for her to do heavy chores, and Mama is afraid she won't find a husband. Why would the police shoot a gun at a little girl unless they had violence in their own hearts?

I don't know as anyone here wants to get violent. It's the coal company police that gets restless with their guns and their clubs.

As for getting along with no wages, we're doing all right. We still got our chickens and our ducks and we can trade eggs with the Horvaths next door who have got a milk-cow. Also, Tadek and Stepan pick up all the loose feathers every day from the ducks and chickens. With feathers of the goose we had at Christmas time and the duck and chicken feathers we will soon have enough to stuff a feather bed because we have saved feathers now three years. That will be good for Mama when Billy comes to be born.

From

Frank Kovacs

Frank

P.S. Mila asked me to read this letter to her because she saw her name in it, and she says the same thing I said, which is why would coal company police shoot at a girl if they didn't have badness in their hearts?

To find out more about the Great Coal Strike of 1902, visit winslowpress.com.

59

June 7, 1902

The White House

Dear Frank,

This is precisely why I disapprove of strikes! Tempers flare. And as you say, men with guns become restless. I'm very sorry to hear your sister was wounded in that manner. What a dreadful thing to happen to a little girl. Perhaps the coal companies are not as careful as they should be in whom they hire for their police forces. There is never a reason for firing at a crowd of women and children.

I hear John Mitchell is a fine fellow and will do the right thing by the miners. Put your trust in him. I am sure he will be able to negotiate with the coal companies. Meanwhile, you should be prepared to go back to work. I think it is the best thing.

Sincerely,

Theodore Roosevelt

Theodore Roosevelt

Guards protecting railway cars from striking miners.

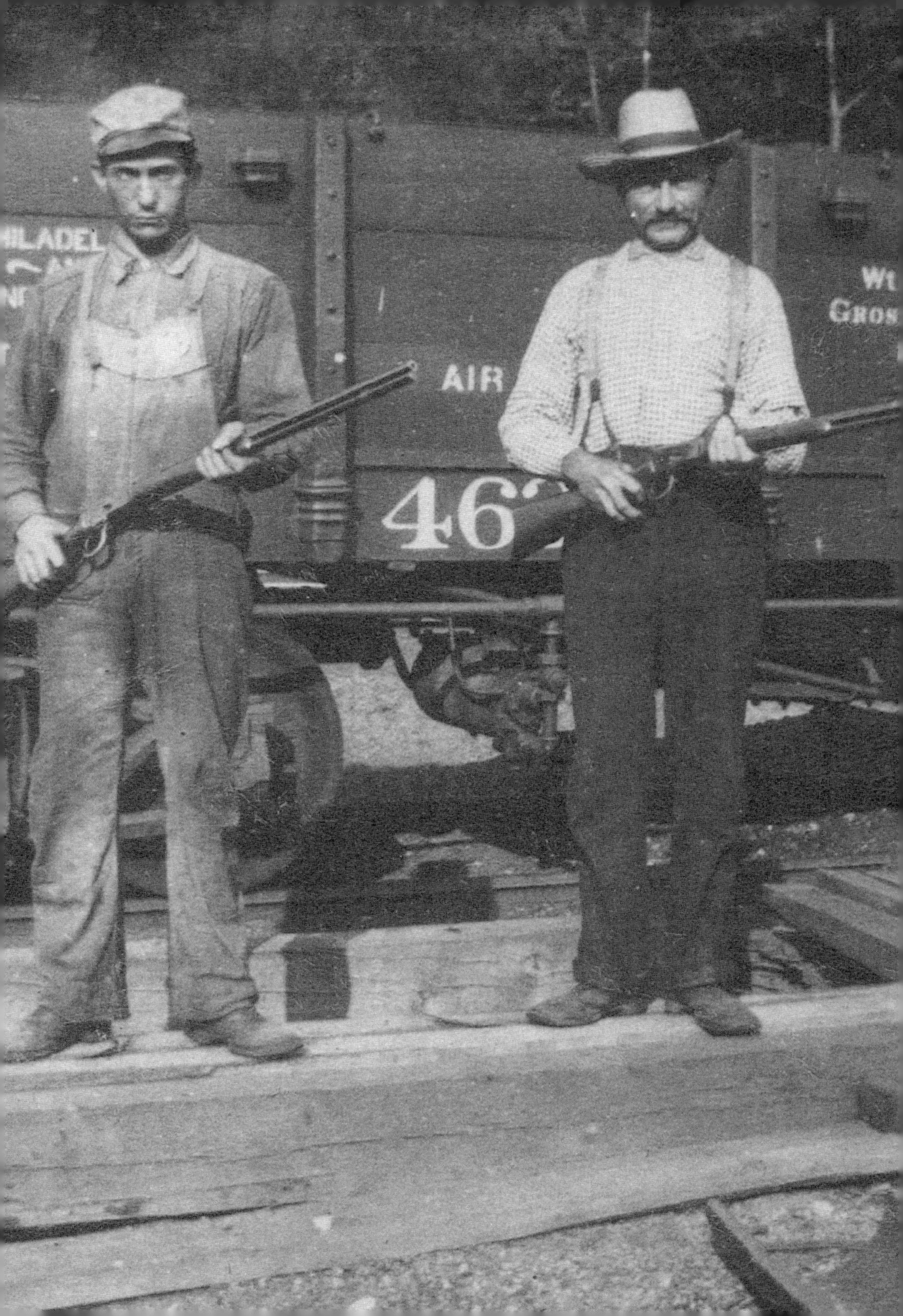

HILADEL
AIR
462
Wt
GROS

Oneida, Pennsylvania

Dear Mr. Roosevelt,

   They say Johnny Mitchell can't get nowhere with the mine owners and they don't even give him the time of day. What I heard was this: the fellow that runs the Reading Railroad says us Slavic miners don't suffer. I guess he thinks we ain't even human. Here there is a lady with the name of Mother Jones. She does lead many protest marches to keep the mines shut down. She says always to be strong and stand up for what's right.

   A lot of folks is leaving the coal patch. Also some folks is being kicked out of their houses by the sheriff. People getting on trains going anywhere but here. I hear some folks is even heading back to the old country. I can't believe that. There's got to be some other good jobs here in this country without going back.

   We Kovacs plan to stay put. Mila and Janka keep picking coal from the culm heaps to sell. Me and my little brothers are keeping an eye on the huckleberries growing on the hills. When they get ripe we aim to pick as many as we can and sell them.

   I am proud of the miners.

Frank Kovacs

From Frank Kovacs

These coal-patch women are picking culm from the culm heap.

Sagamore Hill, New York

Dear Frank,

I like your spirit, young man. Bully for you! Your pride does you credit. And I'm glad your family intends to stay put. I wouldn't want to be chased out of my home because of some pig-headed mine owners, either. Keep a level head and this problem will soon be resolved. I won't scold you any longer.

As for huckleberries: when they're good and ready, send some to me here at our house on Long Island. We've got a crowd of cousins who like nothing better on their pancakes. I'll see to it you get a money order in payment.

Affectionately your friend,

Theodore Roosevelt

Theo. Roosevelt

Quentin picking daisies at Sagamore Hill.

July 2, 1902

Oneida, Pennsylvania

Dear Mr. President,

  I saw yesterday's newspaper when
I was looking for something to wrap
around these berry boxes. It said it
was the anniversary of a ride you
took somewhere named San Juan Hill.
I guess you was always a famous man
even before you become president,
if they're making anniversaries out
of horseback rides. I do go to the
barbershop back of the company store
to find the old newspapers that the
men finish to reading. It's only the

bachelors
go to the
barber
shop. The
men that
has wives
or mothers
get their
hairs cut
to home.
Stepan has
not his

hairs ever been cut yet and he does look sometime like a little girl but Janka and Mila always say Mama not to cut it, he is the angel. I told them he won't be such a angel when he does go work at the mine on account of angels stays clean and white, do you remember I did tell you that joke?

I hope you like the berries. My brothers and me picked them although Tadek, I mean Ted, to be American ate one for each one he put in the box. Elsewise we would have got more. They're in his stomach. Mama says the best way to eat huckleberries is in a pie, and she begs your pardon if you already did know that. Also they make a very good jam.

Your friend,

Frank Kovacs

Frank

P.S. Happy Fourth of July in two days.

Theodore Roosevelt, dressed up in his rough rider uniform.

To find out more about the Rough Riders at San Juan Hill, visit winslowpress.com.

July 7, 1902

Sagamore Hill, Long Island

Dear Frank,

The huckleberries arrived only a little squashed, but my pack of wild savages (by that I mean my children and their cousins) descended upon them with cries and whoops more bloodcurdling than anything I've ever heard. Mrs. Roosevelt tried to preserve some for the kitchen, but it was no use. Eli, the macaw, got loose during the fray and tried gobbling as many as he could, and defended his rights with his terrible beak, which I believe is strong enough to bite through a stove-lid. The dogs, Sailor Boy and Jack, naturally thought something first rate was happening and took the chance to jump onto the table. Thankfully Jonathan (the rat) and the flying squirrel were occupied elsewhere, or no doubt they would have joined the fight, too. We are all most appreciative of the huckleberries, but for the safety of all concerned, we'd better not have any more!

And thank you, we had a tremendous Fourth of July celebration here, with rockets and firecrackers and sailing races on the Sound. I then led the children on a good long ramble, and everyone got thoroughly covered with mud, which is the way they all like it best. We wear as few clothes as decency allows on these hikes, and tramp through the woods to a pond that we swim across in our clothes, then we walk across to Cold Spring Harbor, swim across to the beach

at our cousin's house, then slog our way across a marsh before we come back home to get clean and dry.

Ethel came along too, of course, and speaking of haircuts, the poor girl nearly had a catastrophe. In scrambling through some tall weeds, she got terribly tangled in some burdocks, which have a dreadful sort of prickle-ball. Her hair was so snarled up with burdocks that her mother threatened to cut it all off. Only great patience with the comb saved the girl's pretty hair. Our young cousin Eleanor Roosevelt was the one who so diligently untangled Ethel's head; Eleanor is not quite stalwart enough to come on our mad scrambles (and does not swim), but she is a good sweet girl. She is often rather timid when I play "bear" with the children. She hasn't had as ferocious an upbringing as my Little Bears have.

As for the newspapers recognizing the anniversary of my ride up San Juan Hill, well, it was a bully charge against the Spaniards in Cuba, and we gave them a thrashing. So in all modesty, I must say, it wasn't an ordinary horseback ride.

Thank you once again for the excellent berries, and I hope your local bank will honor this check.

Your friend,

Theodore Roosevelt

Theodore Roosevelt

July 14, 1902

Oneida, Pennsylvania

Dear Mr. Roosevelt,

I reckon I should have sent more berries the first time, and I am sorry that now you don't want no more. Too bad that our Ted ate so many. I guess I know what it's like to have a big clamor over a small amount of good food. If ain't Mama or Papa looking, me and my brothers and sisters will fight over food just like cats and dogs. But if one of them is around, we have to go a particular order: first Papa gets his food, then us brothers, then the sisters, then Mama goes last. I don't know if that's the way all folks do it, but that's how we do it here. The potatoes ain't ready to dig, yet we got to let them get bigger. Tadek, his job now is to go through the potato patch with a can of

kerosene for to kill them potato bugs.
The bugs, they do eat the leafs of the
potato plants and make the potatoes
weak so we must knock the bugs off the
leafs into the kerosene that kills them.

We do get plenty of milk now from
Horvaths. Even Mama is drinking that
milk. But our stomachs is getting a
might hollow.

But it ain't no use complaining. We
miners got to stick together. All us
families is trying to share around.
Some folks is talking about going back
to work, and they don't want to keep
at the strike, but we won't break this
strike. Mother Jones does come around
and say to the people be brave.
There's plenty of men that'll keep
anyone from going back into the mines.
I know this.

From

Frank

Frank Kovacs, Son of a Miner

P.S. Thank you for payment on them berries although it
was a mite too much. We paid our rent with that money.
At the store they did give me the money for that check
and said how could I get money from the president so I
said to them I sold you berries. They had very much
surprise.

---

*Mother Jones, whose real name was Mary Harris, worked
tirelessly on behalf of the striking workers.*

**To learn out more about Mother
Jones, visit winslowpress.com.**

July 31, 1902

The White House

Dear Frank,

What a terrible thing this is that has happened! An innocent man killed by a riotous mob in Shenandoah! I have had a telephone call from the governor of Pennsylvania, and told him I heartily approved his decision to call out the militia.

Frank, heed me well! Stay out of the mobs! No good can come of this kind of hysterical action. If the miners choose to stop work, they must still abide by law and order or else suffer the consequences.

This is a great, great tragedy. I must write to poor Mr. Beddal's family.

From

Theodore Roosevelt

Theodore Roosevelt

John Mitchell became president of the United Mine Workers Union in 1898 at the age of 29. He was known as the "boy president."

Oneida Pennsylvania

Dear Mr. President,

I hate to tell you this but I was there and I seen it all. There was some fellows coming back from the West Shenandoah mine with a deputy sheriff name of Tom Beddal, only they wasn't wearing work clothes. When they got to the Reading depot, some strikers asked them what they was carrying inside them bundles they had, and sure enough, it was work clothes. I did not see how the fight started exactly. But it was pretty soon a brawl all over the depot. The deputy sheriff, that Tom Beddal, he was blazing away with his pistol and then locked himself inside the express office.

That was when that fellow's brother, him what had the hardware store so they say, Joe Beddal, he tried to go help his brother, but some a them strikers thought he was bringing more guns and bullets and such, and he got attacked. Then the rest of the police from the town shows up. I seen a lot of this from the roof of a barbering shop, where I climbed up. But then some of us men from Oneida figures we'd better get out of the fight before there's a lot of shooting.

And I am saying prayers now for that Joe Beddal that died from his wounds. This strike is a bad thing, but we can't give up now. I feel confused in my head about it, but my heart says we can't give up.

Frank Kovacs

From Frank Kovacs

August 11, 1902

The White House

Dear Frank,

    I write with a heavy heart. It looks quite certain that we shall not resolve this conflict speedily or painlessly. It is clear that you and your fellow miners are already suffering. Innocent bystanders such as poor Mr. Beddal are suffering, and now the newspapers have gotten wind of the seriousness of the situation. They are now full of dire predictions about how the country will fare through the winter if the strike remains at a standstill.

    My son, Kermit, was looking over the newspapers with me at the breakfast table, and remarked on the coal strike and then asked me, "Are you still writing to that miner boy in Pennsylvania who is my same age?" I told him I was, and reported on your circumstances. After some thought he pointed out that you may possibly find it difficult to get to the post office if you are busy with extra chores, and he has given me these stamps for your use and says you're welcome to them as he finds he doesn't have so many letters to write as he expected to this summer.

Your friend,

Theodore Roosevelt

Theodore Roosevelt

Cartoonist Herbert Johnson showed that while owners were fighting miners, makers of coal substitutes such as natural gas threatened to overtake the coal business.

August 18, 1902

Oneida Pennsylvania

Dear Mr. President,

Please tell Kermit I am obliged to him. I know he aims to spare me any shame for taking charity and that's how come he put it that way. It ain't lack of time, it's lack of work that's the problem here.

The union men say it's one of the hardest things in striking that you got to take handouts sometimes. But that is what the union dues is for so we can have some strike pay. It ain't handouts really.

We keep doing what we have to do to get along. The ducks is almost all sold except for one that was Janka's favorite. It has the name of Kachka which only means duck in Polish language. I said her it has to have a real name but Janka says duck is its real name. When it was still in the egg she called that one Jajko which only means egg in Polish language. This is what kind of girl is Janka.

There is a couple or three bands from the coal patch what it going on concert tour in the big cities. There's the Lithuanian band from Shenandoah and one from St. Joseph Polish Roman Catholic at Mt. Carmel and I think maybe an other. They put on a concert of songs and dancing from the old country with the old-time dresses and such that they still have, and I hear they been making plenty of money for the strike fund.

But what we really do want is for to get the strike over and we can go back to working but we can't end that strike if we don't get some changes what we asked for. Until we do we have to stay on strike and take the handouts and swallow our pride.

But tell Kermit I am much obliged.

With gratefulness,

Frank Kovacs

Frank Kovacs

To learn more about Slavic folk dancing and music, go to winslowpress.com.

77

The White House

Dear Frank,

I'll be leaving here soon on a speaking tour. I shall be in Massachusetts, and then will be heading to the middle West. Please continue to write and tell me how all the miners in the coalpatch are making out, but I may not receive your letters until I return.

I always leave on these tours of mine with a mixture of sadness at leaving my family, eagerness to meet my fellow Americans, and curiosity to know what strange gifts people will foist upon me. I have acquired a reputation for keeping an absolute menagerie of animals, and well-wishers are always presenting me with creatures. In addition to beasts such as the zebra and the hyena which the Emperor of Ethiopia sent me, ordinary citizens are in the habit of giving me snakes, lizards, owls, bear cubs, flying squirrels, eagles, coyotes, etc. Some of these I have gladly kept as pets for the children (including, for some time, a black bear we called Jonathan Edwards because he seemed to resemble that devout minister). However, some of the gifts are inconvenient to have at home, to say the least. We are obliged to send these to the Zoo. I can't help but wonder what creeping, crawling, running or flying thing I will be presented with on this expedition!

Your friend,

Theodore Roosevelt

Theodore Roosevelt

P.S. I cannot for the life of me figure out how to pronounce "Jajko".

To learn more about the "Zoo" at the White House, go to winslowpress.com.

Roosevelt with his four sons. (left to right) *Kermit, Quentin, Ted, Jr.,* and *Archie.*

September 4, 1902

Oneida, PA

Dear Mr. President,

I read it in the paper, they say you were in a terrible accident in Massachusetts. I seen them trolley cars once when I went to Scranton. They must be some dangerous machines to wreck your buggy that way and kill a man. Did you get hurt real bad? I'm shamed to say it, but some of the miners here is angry at you for getting injured because now they say it will take the president to talk some sense into the coal companies and if you ain't well, we can't count on you.

But that's not my opinion.

Frank

Frank Kovacs

P.S. Did you ever hear some person say in surprise yipes? That's how that Jajko is to be said. Yiko. Very many words in Polish language use same sound but different letter from American language. Kachka that used to be Jajko is getting very fat and Mama wants to cook him. Janka is a good girl, she will not say no to Mama. But she is very sad to say goodbye to her bird. I wish he could only go to a zoo but he is for food.

To learn more about trolley cars, **go to** winslowpress.com.

Mother Jones was impatient with the slow pace of negotiations. Here she stands with workers outside a mine entrance.

22 Jackson Place
Washington D.C.
Dear Frank,

Perhaps it was prophetic that you named your broken-legged rat Roosevelt. The doctors tell me I'm lucky to be alive. The wound I sustained in the dreadful accident in Pittsfield became abscessed, and by the time I reached Indianapolis my leg was so swollen and painful that it had to be drained to prevent blood poisoning. I insisted on watching the operation, naturally. During the war in Cuba I witnessed my fair share of battlefield surgery, and I'm not a squeamish man. They gave me a local anesthetic and went to work draining the wound to prevent blood poisoning. They say I'm to keep off my leg for weeks, but that is not possible. I'm a man of action and I will not be hobbled!

As we've got remodeling going on at the White House, the children have all been sent to Oyster Bay, and Mrs. Roosevelt and I are living across the street for the time being. Rumors have been circulating that my pack of wild children have actually destroyed the interior of the executive mansion with their indoor pony rides and roller-skating and stiltwalking, and tobogganing down the stairs on tin serving trays, and that is why the remodeling is required. I refuse to comment on these rumors beyond saying that the White House was long overdue for modernization anyway. This is the twentieth century, after all, and we must keep up with the times.

Alice Roosevelt posing with a pet parrot, one of the many pets that caused such chaos at The White House.

Incidentally, I was in Indianapolis to give a speech to veterans of the Spanish-American war, and quite a few people asked me what my position on the coal strike was. Indianapolis, Chicago, and Detroit all have considerable populations of new citizens from Poland, Bohemia, Slovakia, Lithuania, Moravia and Slovenia, and they tell me that the fraternal orders and societies are sending aid to their brethren in the coal patch. Bully for them, I say. They show good fellow feeling.

Meanwhile, rest assured that the situation in Pennsylvania is much on my mind. I have sent cables to all the coal company owners, and to Mr. Mitchell, requesting that they come to see me. You will not be surprised to hear that Mr. Mitchell declares himself ready to come at a moment's notice. You will also not be surprised to hear that the coal companies are dragging their feet. But by thunder! They will not refuse to meet with the president!

We'll resolve this as quickly as possible, Frank. I promise you. I may be off my feet, but I'm not off the job.

I feel very sorry for your sister, Janka. All of my children are very fond of animals and as you know, we have a great many pets in our household even after sending so many to the Zoo. It would grieve them very much if we had to eat one of them.

Sincerely,

Theodore Roosevelt

Theo. Roosevelt

Cartoonist Homer Davenport depicted an industry that made its profits by starving and endangering its workers.

October 1, 1902

Oneida, Pennsylvania

Dear Mr. Roosevelt,

I'm that sorry about your leg. Did I ever say to you what happened to Roosevelt? That rat I mean. Well when we all walked out of the mine and brought the mules out, I remembered to run back in and see if I could find that old gimpy rat. I was setting there waiting for the shaft elevator to catch a ride down, and when the cage rises up I seen that Roosevelt riding up on the top of the cage. I figure he was going on strike too. His leg was healed up pretty good by then so I guess he must be doing all right. I hope he decides to look for other work and not go back to the mines when they open again.

Folks here is wondering if we'll have to stay on strike over winter. We had some frost here this morning and more girls than normal is out picking the culm heaps because we know it's going to get real cold here soon. I made each of my sisters a split oak basket to make carrying the coal easier. I guess city kids isn't so lucky as we are since at least we got the culm heaps nearby and we can sift it for coal to burn. I expect folks are getting upset thinking they'll be cold this winter. I hope when they do get some coal they'll think on the miner that brought it up out of the ground. Some of the Irish folks over at Shepton got evicted yesterday and all their worldly goods is on the street. Strike already lasted too long for lots of miner families.

We dug our potatoes anyway. They got good and big and we filled up the whole space under Mila and Jankas bed.

My Mama heard me say by thunder and said she thought it was cussing, but I told her you say it all the time and if the president can say it, it ain't cussing.

I ain't at all surprised to hear that Johnny Mitchell is wanting to play fair and square with you. We got a picture of Johnny Mitchell that we tore out of a newspaper up on our wall. I hope you do get them coal owners to set down with you, by thunder.

From Frank Kovacs

Frank Kovacs

P.S. This is next day. We have very much surprise here. The new baby did come but it is not Billy! It is another little girl. Mama, she say what is name of Mrs. Roosevelt?

October 7, 1902

The White House

Dear Frank,

The coal owners are lucky I am confined to my wheelchair, else I would have thrashed them all down Pennsylvania Avenue and back again. George Baer (who I expect you know is the president of the Reading Railroad) and his colleagues arrived for our meeting in gaudy, fancy carriages, which only served to remind everyone else how much of the profits they have amassed from the coal fields. Your man, Johnny Mitchell, arrived by streetcar, as befits a man of the people. I like him! You're right to place your trust in him, Frank. I have the highest opinion of him.

I cannot say the same of the coal company representatives: on the contrary, I have the lowest opinion of them. Their manner was insolent in the extreme. If the matter had not been so very important, I would have terminated the meeting and sent them packing. They seem to think that giving the miners better pay would cause such a rise in the price of coal as to be intolerable for the public. What they apparently have never given a moment's thought to, is that perhaps they should be willing to take a smaller profit from the mines, rather than shift the increase on to the public. It makes my blood boil to see them in their fine clothes saying they have the best interests of the public at heart, and therefore cannot give the miners an increase.

George F. Baer, president of the Reading Railroad, which owned many of the coal mines, is known for having said of miners "They don't suffer. Why, they can't even speak English."

As you know by now, because it has been in the papers since yesterday, I had to declare the Pennsylvania militia ready to do service in the anthracite fields: we must have the coal, Frank. The country will be crippled without it! You know our factories will grind to a halt, and our citizens in the colder climes of the nation will suffer come winter. But I also swear that if the miners will return to work, I will appoint a commission of inquiry to examine just how the coal companies have been operating and force the companies to abide by the findings.

The company representatives, led by that scoundrel Baer, claimed that the majority of miners did wish to return to the mines, but were kept away by the terror tactics of a violent minority. They asserted that it is only this "minority" that is agitating for changes. Even without your letters proving him a liar, I would have known him to be false. A man of Baer's stripe would never admit that anyone has cause for complaint. I tell you, Frank, I could have kicked that man down the stairs if I'd been able to stand up. I am almost tempted to seize control of the mines in the name of the United States government. He and his kind would deserve it.

Don't give up hope, Frank. We're working as hard as we can.

As for your joyful news: tell your father congratulations from the President and Mrs. Roosevelt, whose Christian name is Edith. We both wish your mother and the new baby girl the best health and happiness. We adore babies.

Your friend,

Theodore Roosevelt

Theodore Roosevelt

Oneida, Pennsylvania

Dear Mr. President,

Well, the union voted, and it was what they call unanimous. To a man they agreed to keep on at the strike. It figures the owners would say us miners is afraid to go to work on account of a few violent fellers, but that is horsewash. It's our decision to stick with the strike until we get our fair shakes.

I ain't so sure what to make of these soldiers coming down here and saying they are going to work the mines. What do they know about mines and mules and workings and such? Everyone agrees as how the commission you want to name some fellas to is a good idea. Only make sure that commission is fair and ain't just a bunch of rich folks that never got their hands dirty. Make sure there is a working man.

Believe me, there ain't nobody wants this strike over more than us. But we got to hold the line. Well go back to work when Johnny Mitchell says we should.

Sincerely,

Frank Kovacs

Frank

P.S. Mama and Papa they have given the name Catherine Edith Kovacs to our new sister.

Coal company representatives resisted the miners' demands until they were forced to give in.

October 22, 1902

The White House

Dear Frank,

God bless the union men! I am so relieved the men voted to go back to work. You have my solemn vow that this Anthracite Coal Strike Commission will do its level best to study the conditions of the miners, and they will return a fair and honest report. You'll get your fair shakes, Frank.

Kermit will be very glad to know that this is resolved. He is away at school in Massachusetts, now, but continues to ask about you in his letters. My regret is that you will be returning to your difficult and dreary labors underground instead of pursuing the education you so well deserve.

At the moment, I am playing nursemaid to Ethel's two guinea pigs, as she is out and fears the small creatures will not be safe unless I keep a watchful eye on them. They are cuddled in a basket near the radiator, which is warm as toast.

I am at this moment picturing Catherine Edith in a basket, too, snug as a guinea pig. God bless you all.

Your friend,

Theodore Roosevelt

Theodore Roosevelt

John Mitchell at his desk, from which he kept a lively correspondence with Mother Jones.

Oneida, Pennsylvania

Dear Mr. President,

   I am back at work and I got to break in some new mules. My heart feels good to see the long lines of men walking to the mines in the morning with their lunch pails and their tools. It's dark in the mornings when we leave for work, and there's a right frosty bite in the air but you can hear folks laughing and singing in the darkness. My papa is a fire boss now at Oneida Number 2, and I believe our wages together will be enough so my brothers and sisters can stick in school a mite longer and not have to go work. I will be happy to see them get more educating than I had.

   Next to our picture of Johnny Mitchell we now got a picture of my friend Theodore Roosevelt up on the wall.

Thank you.

Frank Kovacs

Frank Kovacs, Working man

Oneida Pennsylvania

Dear Mr. Roosevelt,

I hope you do remember me. I wish to say you Happy Christmas, or Wesołych Świąt as we say in Polish language. We are back working in the mine and hoping for good news from the Coal Commission to set us right.

May your New Year have health and fortune to you and your family.

Frank (Kovacs)

The White House

Dear Frank,

    Of course I remember you.
Thank you for your kind New Year's wishes.
I think you can rely on the Coal Commission
to do right by you, and so I think I can promise
you health and fortune in this new year, too.

    My regards to your father and mother.
I trust the new baby is doing well and
prospering.

Sincerely,

Theodore Roosevelt

March 23, 1903

Oneida Pennsylvania

Dear Mr. President,

  This is a good decision and we are satisfactory with it. We have pay raise by ten percent of what we have now and eight hours work day. Also, the workers who do weighing of the coal cars now are paid by miners instead of company. Do you see this makes them better at weighing! Instead of coal company paying them to weigh the cars light, now miners pays them to way the cars at true weight. This is a good change for miners. Soon in maybe two years I will be miner too on account of I am big and very strong and will make ever better wage for my family. New baby Catherine Edith is very favorite baby in this town Oneida. People say when Catherine Edith come, that is the end of strike. So she is good luck baby.

  God bless the union. Soon it will have official standing and the miners will always have a friend.

Sincerely,

Frank

Frank

More about Theodore Roosevelt

In 1901, when this fictional correspondence begins, Theodore Roosevelt had only been President of the United States for seven days. On September 13th, 1901, President William McKinley was shot by an assassin while on a visit to Buffalo, New York. The next day, McKinley died of his wounds, and his Vice President, Theodore ("Teddy") Roosevelt, took the oath of office, becoming America's twenty-sixth president.

Although the story of the friendship between President Roosevelt and Frank Kovacs is invented, it isn't difficult to imagine Teddy Roosevelt taking such a personal interest in a young man he didn't even know. An outgoing and curious man, Roosevelt was the father of six children of his own, and some people considered him to be something of a big kid himself. The story of Roosevelt's childhood and the story of his relationship with his own children tell us something about what kind of person he was.

Young Theodore Roosevelt

Theodore Roosevelt, Jr. was born in New York in 1858. His father, Theodore Sr. (known as "Greatheart"), was the son of one of New York City's richest men. His mother, Martha ("Mittie"), came from a wealthy Georgia family. Teddy, whose childhood nickname was "Teedie," had an older sister, Anna. He was soon followed by a brother, Elliott, and then by another sister, Corinne.

Theodore, Sr. was an importer and philanthropist who was extremely well thought of in New York. He was known

Attends Columbia Law School but drops out to pursue politics.

Member of the New York State Assembly.

Wife Alice dies after giving birth to their daughter (also named Alice).

for his honesty, his strong beliefs, and for his social conscience and generosity. Although Theodore, Sr. was a businessman, he wasn't interested in the business for its own sake. He thought of it as a way of supporting his many charitable projects. Children—all children, not just his own—were important to Mr. Roosevelt, and so many of his projects benefited the children of New York. He funded all kinds of organizations, large and small, to help educate and care for the city's young people. He also established and funded the Children's Aid Society, which is still in existence. It was this kind of work that caused him to be known as Greatheart.

Mr. Roosevelt also participated in the creation of two New York museums that are among the most important in this country: the Metropolitan Museum of Art, and the American Museum of Natural History. The charter for the Museum of Natural History was approved at a meeting in the Roosevelt family parlor in 1869, when Teedie was eleven years old.

As a young child, Teedie had severe asthma, and was often sick. He was quiet and shy, and something of a loner. And, like many shy and quiet people, he was a careful observer of the world around him. His greatest pleasures included watching birds and animals. By the time he was ten he had already started his own natural history "museum" at home—it contained over a hundred specimens, carefully labeled and organized by Teedie himself. He was fascinated by animal behavior and spent a lot of time drawing and writing about what he observed.

Reading was highly valued in the Roosevelt household, and Teedie and his siblings read many books. Mr. Roosevelt

Alice
(1884–1980)

Theodore Jr.
(1887–1944)

encouraged his children to be curious and to ask questions.
The Roosevelt children never had formal schooling until they
went off to college, and so they were dependent on each other
for companionship. Anna, Teedie, Elliott and Corinne were very
close as children and remained so as adults. As he grew older,
Teedie was more and more physically active, even though he
still had asthma. He went hiking and climbing with his brother
and sisters, and played in the woods during the summer.

The Roosevelts lived in the style of wealthy New Yorkers
of the 1800s, with large city and country houses, many servants,
and lots of travel. Mr. Roosevelt wanted to expose his children
to other cultures and ways of life. Part of the children's
education included extensive travel in Europe and Africa.

In 1869, the family took a one-year "grand tour" of Europe,
from Liverpool to Berlin to Venice, with many stops in between.
During this journey, Teedie's asthma often returned, and
sometimes the attacks were so severe that the family's travel
plans had to be changed. Despite his illness, Teedie kept
detailed journals of the entire trip. These journals reflect his
constant interest in the natural world, and also his eye for the
little things. From dogs to castles, he wrote down as much as
he could about what he did and saw. He was always excited
about discovering new things.

Several years later, the family would take another extended
trip overseas—this time, they spent two months sailing 1200
miles down the Nile. With his mother and siblings, Teedie also
traveled through the Suez Canal, the Holy Land, and visited the
city of Constantinople.

The summer of 1872, right before his trip down the Nile,

 **Kermit**
(1889–1943)

 **Ethel**
(1891–1977)

 Archibald
(1894–1979)

was an important one for Teddy Roosevelt. He got his first pair of glasses, and discovered how much of the world he hadn't been seeing. Glasses "opened up the world to me," he wrote later. "I had no idea how beautiful the world was." Having better eyesight increased his confidence, socially and physically. Teddie was less shy and more active, and went on to develop the outgoing, boisterous character we associate with him today.

After graduating from Harvard in 1880, Roosevelt married his first wife, Alice Hathaway Lee, and moved back to New York City to attend Columbia Law School. It was during this time that he began to take an active interest in politics, stopping on his way home from classes to hang out and argue with members of a republican club that met over a neighborhood saloon. Although politics was considered inappropriate for someone of Theodore's social class, it was far more exciting to him than any of his law school studies were, and he soon joined the club. In the fall of 1881, some members of the Republican Club decided that Theodore would make an excellent candidate for the New York state legislature.

Roosevelt took little convincing, and was elected as an assemblyman, winning almost twice the number of votes as his opponent. He was the youngest assemblyman ever to serve in New York state. This was the beginning of a successful political career that would take him from the legislature to the governor's mansion and eventually to the White House, where he would be the youngest man (at that time) ever to become President of the United States.

Quentin
(1897–1918)

(Quentin's death in WWI
was a crushing blow to
his father.)

1895-1897

President of the
New York City
Police Board.

1897-1898

Assistant Secretary
of the Navy under
President William
McKinley.

Roosevelt the Dad

By the time he moved into the White House in 1901,
Theodore Roosevelt had six children of his own. Alice,
Theodore Jr., Kermit, Ethel, Archibald, and Quentin had
close relationships with their father. Teddy was a loving
and playful father who took a great interest in everything
his children did. He encouraged them in their different
hobbies and interests, even the ones that might have driven
another parent crazy. For example, the Roosevelt children
were always acquiring pets of all kinds, from ponies to
parrots to badgers, and these pets often had the run of the
White House. (Teddy really did baby-sit his daughter's
guinea pigs in the Oval Office, as he writes to Frank in
this book.)

While he encouraged his children to spend time out-
doors and take part in games and sports, Teddy had never
lost his love of reading, and he passed that love on to his
family. The Roosevelt children were known as "great readers." Because the president was often separated from his
children during his travels, he kept in close touch with
them by writing letters. His many letters to his family are
full of stories and little drawings as well as questions about
their pets and activities. Teddy enjoyed accompanying the
kids on their expeditions around the Roosevelt home in
Oyster Bay, Long Island (Sagamore Hill), especially if they
involved camping. He was often the only grown-up in a
crowd of children.

1898	1898–1900	1900

Serves as colonel of the "Rough Riders" volunteer cavalry regiment during the Spanish-American War.

Governor of New York.

Nominated as President McKinley's running mate at the Republican National Convention.

President Theodore Roosevelt and the Anthracite Strike

At the turn of the century, one of the East coast's primary fuels was a hard, clean-burning coal called anthracite. Many of the anthracite mines were located in the eastern part of Pennsylvania, where entire towns had developed around the coal industry. It was mostly immigrants from eastern and southern Europe (countries including Poland, Slovakia, Hungary, and Italy) who worked in these mines.

For the miners and their families, conditions were rough. There were no enforced safety regulations in the mines, and anthracite miners were paid very poorly. Out of their tiny incomes, miners had to pay the mining companies back for such things as rent on their company-owned homes and the cost of oil for the lamps they used underground. Often the mines charged more than the miners earned, leaving miners owing the company money. Anthracite miners made an average salary of less than $600 a year, and most of that money went right back to the companies. Miners worked long, hard hours underground, breathing in coal dust that made many of them ill. They worked an average of twelve hours a day and only had one day off, Sunday. In 1901, the year that Theodore Roosevelt became President, 111 anthracite mine workers were killed on the job.

In May of 1902, Roosevelt had been in office for barely eight months when almost 150,000 members of the United Mine Workers Union went on strike in an effort to get better pay and better working conditions. The union had demanded a

Serves as Vice President under McKinley; becomes President when McKinley is assassinated.

The White House undergoes extensive renovations and reconstruction, including the addition of the West Wing.

substantial increase in pay, and changes in some of the unfair company practices that harmed miners. The mine operators refused to recognize the union, and one of them, the president of the Reading Railroad, said this about the mostly-immigrant miners: "They don't suffer. Why, they can't even speak English."

The public supported the miners, and since most of the cities and industries on the East coast were heated and fueled by anthracite, it was of great importance to everyone that the strike be resolved. As the summer of 1902 ended and cold weather approached, the miners were still on strike. President Roosevelt, who hadn't been involved in the negotiations, realized just how serious the situation was. In some states, schools were closing because of the lack of fuel. The government expected riots.

Roosevelt was frustrated by the lack of progress with the strike, and this is one of the main reasons he became involved. His goal was to protect the public, since he believed that the interests of the public came first, and after that the interests of the workers and company owners. At the end of September, he invited the United Mine Workers' union leaders and the mine operators to come to the White House for a meeting to try and work things out. He was the first American president to directly intervene in a labor dispute.

John Mitchell, the head of the UMW, joined other union leaders and some of the mine operators at the White House on October 3, 1902. By the end of this meeting, Roosevelt was shocked by the selfishness of the mine operators and decided that, if necessary, he would send 10,000 federal troops into Pennsylvania to seize the mines and run them *his* way. He ordered the troops to stand by. This threat, combined with

Roosevelt's administration
recognizes the new country
of Panama as it declares its
independence (in a revolution
encouraged by TR) from
Colombia, and construction
of the Panama Canal begins.

Establishes the first
national wildlife refuge
(at Pelican Island,
in Florida).

Runs for the presidency
and is elected to a
second term.

secret negotiations by the Secretary of State, convinced the mine operators to do things Roosevelt's way. They agreed that if the miners would go back to work, the operators would cooperate with a commission that would decide what kinds of wages and changes the miners would receive.

Over three months, hearings were held in Pennsylvania, and in the end the miners won a shorter day (eight hours) and a ten percent increase in their wages. They didn't get everything they wanted—the mine operators were not required to recognize the union, for example—but it was a start.

Theodore Roosevelt's strong opinions and passionate feelings about justice helped to resolve the anthracite strike. Even those who didn't agree with him (then or in the future) saw that he was not the kind of person who would stand by and watch what he perceived as injustice. If you were a kid like Frank Kovacs, you would want him on your side.

Two years after the strike, Roosevelt would take a role in negotiating another dispute—this time, the Russo-Japanese War. He brought representatives of both Russia and Japan to Portsmouth, New Hampshire, where they had the peace and quiet they needed to work out a peace agreement that ended the war. For his role as mediator in these negotiations, Theodore Roosevelt was the first American to be awarded the Nobel Peace Prize.

Among the important events that occurred during Roosevelt's presidency was the 1903 treaty with Panama that granted the United States permanent use of a zone along the Panama Canal. Construction of the Canal began that year, and

Acts as mediator in peace negotiations between Russia and Japan, bringing representatives of both countries to New Hampshire to create a peace agreement ending the Russo-Japanese War.

Becomes the first American ever awarded a Nobel Peace Prize (for his efforts in mediating the Russo-Japanese War). Established the first national monument, Devil's Tower National Monument, in Northeast Wyoming.

although it was not completed until 1914, Roosevelt regarded it as one of his most stellar presidential achievements.

In 1906, Roosevelt supported two major pieces of legislation, the Meat Inspection Act and the Pure Food and Drug Act, that were created to protect Americans from spoiled or polluted foods. These laws provided for government inspection of meat and helped create government standards for the labeling, packaging, and sale of foods and drugs.

As president, one of Theodore Roosevelt's nicknames was "the Great Conservationist." Not surprisingly, he used his powers as president to promote the conservation of America's natural resources, pushing Congress to adopt legislation that would preserve and enhance those resources for generations to come. It was Roosevelt who created the country's first national wildlife refuge on Pelican Island, Florida, in 1903 and its first national monument, the Devil's Head National Monument, in Northeast Wyoming, in 1906. He also set aside millions of acres in national forests and coal lands. With the Land Reclamation Act of 1902, huge dams were constructed out west.
It was during Roosevelt's administration that the White House as we know it today was built. When the large and boisterous Roosevelt family moved into the White House in 1901, they lived in tight, run-down quarters, surrounded by governmental offices.

It was then that major reconstruction began on the White House, expanding the building to include more private space for the president's family and adding an entire wing of executive offices now known as the West Wing.

Leaves the White House and begins a
one-year safari in Africa, collecting
plant and animal specimens for the
Smithsonian Institution.

Runs again for the presidency, but
doesn't win. During the campaign,
is shot in the chest during an attempted
assassination but quickly recovers.

If you are interested in learning more about coal mining, or
about Theodore Roosevelt's life and presidency, please visit
our interactive Web site at winslowpress.com.

Here also is a list of books for further reading.

Books written for kids

Bartoletti, Susan Campbell. *Growing Up in Coal Country*.
New York: Houghton Mifflin, 1996.

Fritz, Jean. *Bully For You, Teddy Roosevelt*. Illustrated by
Mike Wimmer. New York: Putnam Publishing Group, 1991.

Sabin, Louis. *Teddy Roosevelt: Rough Rider*. Mahwah, NJ:
Troll Communications, 1986.

Books written for adults

Brands, H.W. *TR: The Last Romantic*. New York: Basic Books,
1998.

Greene, Victor R. *The Slavic Community on Strike: Immigrant
Labor in Pennsylvania Anthracite*. South Bend, IN: University of
Notre Dame Press, 1968.

McCullough, David. *Mornings on Horseback*. New York: Simon &
Schuster, 1981.

Spends seven months exploring
the "River of Doubt" in Brazil.

Dies of an arterial
blood clot at Sagamore Hill.

Miller, Nathan. *Theodore Roosevelt: A Life*. New York: William
Morrow, 1992.

Morris, Edmund. *The Rise of Theodore Roosevelt*. New York:
Ballantine Books, 1979.

Miller, Donald L. and Richard E. Sharpless. *The Kingdom
of Coal: Work, Enterprise, and Ethnic Communities in the Mine
Fields*. Philadelphia: University of Pennsylvania Press, 1985.

Books that kids and adults can enjoy

Kerr, Joan Paterson. *A Bully Father: Theodore Roosevelt's Letters to
His Children*. New York: Random House, 1995.

Time-Life Editors. *This Fabulous Century, Vol. One (1900–1910)*.
Alexandria, VA: Time-Life Books, 1969.

An original letter of Frank's would have probably looked something like this:

September 20, 1901
Oneida Pennsilvanya

Dear Mr. President,

I herd at work about that President McKinley did got gunned down by a crazy fellow and now you are president in stead of vice president. This is important job. But i do have advise for you dont let no crazy men near you. They is all most all ways trouble. Wishing you health and good luck sir,

Frank Kovacs

Above is a reproduction of an actual letter from Theodore Roosevelt to Ethel, written on June 22, 1904.

About the U.S. Postal Service, *1902*

Frank Kovacs sent his letters to President Roosevelt through the U.S. Postal Service. A two-cent stamp was required on the envelope of an average letter, and although this doesn't seem like very much, it would have been an investment for a young coal miner. Frank might have dropped off his mail at the coal company store, which served as a distribution center. These letters probably traveled by rail between Pennsylvania and Washington, D.C., taking several days to reach their destinations. Mail would be sorted onboard the train and dropped off at local post offices along the way.

United States mail was first transported by railroad in the 1830s, in Frank's home state of Pennsylvania. By 1902, the Post Office had set up a limited delivery service in Minneapolis, Minnesota, using a "horseless wagon." At the time of Frank and President Roosevelt's correspondence, however, railroads were a much faster, more efficient form of transportation.

In 1902, the Post Office also made Rural Free Delivery (RFD) a permanent part of its service. This delivery program allowed mail to be carried and distributed to people living in remote, rural areas. RFD is just one example of how much the country was changing. America was developing systems for moving information and supplies faster than ever before.

Frank Kovac's letters would have been riddled with punctuation, vocabulary, and spelling mistakes, since he had little schooling. In order for his letters to be readable and legible in this book, the spelling has been standardized.

Glossary

anthracite
A special kind of hard, clean-burning coal.

breaker boy
Young boys who worked in the breakers. Their job was to sort the coal as it came from the mine, removing all pieces of rock and slate that had been mixed in.

coal boss
The boss who oversaw the workers. Each section had its own boss. The bosses were known to hit workers with a broom or stick if they were caught daydreaming or were working too slowly.

coal breaker
The place where coal was broken and sorted.

coal chute
This ran from the top of the breaker to the floor. The coal from the mines went down the chutes, where the breaker boys sat ready to sort it.

coal commission
A group that was appointed by the White House to listen to the demands of the workers as well as the coal operators in order to find a way to resolve the strike.

colliery
The coal mine and the buildings around it.

culm heap
Where all the discarded materials from the mines went. People would search the culm heap for pieces of coal that had been mixed in.

fire boss
The term for a coal miner who checked for leaking gas and weak roofs in the mine before the miners started work each day.

mine operators
The people who ran the mines. The public was angry at the mine operators during the strike because the public was not getting coal as a result of the workers being unhappy.

pierogie
Dough filled with meat and vegetables or cheese, which is boiled and then fried.

shaft elevator
A cage-like elevator that took workers down into the mines, 1,200 feet below the ground.

Silesia
A part of Western Poland which no longer exists under that name.

slag
The waste left over after metal was melted.

sprag
Long pieces of wood that the boys, known as "spraggers," used to stop coal cars on the tracks. They did this by sticking the pieces of wood into the wheels of each car.

United Mine Workers Union
Workers joined together in this group to fight against the unfair treatment of miners. They held weekly meetings and organized the strikes of 1900 and 1902.

Index

(Colored numbers represent photographs)

A
anthracite coal, 9, 104
Anthracite Coal Strike Commission, 92, 96

B
Baer, George, 88, 88, 89, 89
breaker, 8, 29, 40, 58
breaker boss, 36
breaker boy, 24, 36, 40

C
carbide lamps, 17, 35
Christmas, 33, 36, 37, 38, 39, 59, 95
coal company, 29, 30, 47, 48, 49, 59, 60, 84, 88, 89, 91, 97, 104
coal miners, family life, 29, 36, 37, 43, 51, 59, 63, 70, 71;
health, 22, 28, 43; living conditions, 9, 36; religion 37, 77;
school, 11, 14, 24; working conditions, 21, 24, 29, 34, 35, 40;
colliery, 14, 15
company store, 29
culm heaps, 29, 42, 62, 63, 86, 87

D
driver, 46

E
Easter, 51
Ellis Island, 11

F
fire boss, 42, 94